Jim and the Monster Party

T0337328

Contents

Written by Catherine Baker

Illustrated by Dusan Pavlic

Collins

What's in this story?

Listen and say

prize

mirror

dragon

jellyfish

The invitation

Jim was at a new school. He didn't know many children in his class. "Don't worry, Jim!" said his mum. "You can make new friends!"

But Jim knew that it wasn't easy to make friends.

Tom was in Jim's class. He often smiled at Jim.
"I would like to be friends with Tom,"
thought Jim.

One day, Tom **invited** Jim to his party.

"Come to my party, Jim!" he said.

"Yes, please!" said Jim. "I would like to come!"

Jim showed the party **invitation** to Mum.

"Fantastic!" said Mum. "It's a monster party!"

"Oh," said Jim. "What's a monster party?"

"People wear monster **costumes**," said Mum. "A monster party has monster food and monster games."

Now Jim was **worried**. He thought about monsters playing games. He thought about monster food.

"I think monster parties are **scary**!" he said.

Jim thought about the food that monsters like to eat. He thought about frog sandwiches and jellyfish ice cream. He thought about green onion milkshakes. He thought about a big monster picnic.

"I wouldn't like to eat monster food!"
thought Jim. "Monster food gives people
a stomach-ache. I could take some cheese
sandwiches to the party."

Jim thought about the games that monsters like playing. He thought about monsters on skateboards. He thought about monsters playing table tennis. He thought about monsters in the playground.

"I can't play monster games!" thought Jim.
"Monster games give people a headache.
I could take my book to the party."

Jim worried about his clothes. Jim didn't want the children at the monster party to laugh at him.

"I don't have a monster costume," he thought. "I don't like monsters!"

That night, Jim couldn't sleep. He was too worried! He thought about all the **problems** with a monster party.

Jim thought, "Do lots of scary monsters go to monster parties?"

The costume

In the morning, Mum looked at Jim.

"What's the matter, Jim?" she asked.

"I'm worried about the monster party.
I don't like monster food or monster games.
And I don't have a monster costume!"

Mum smiled. "Don't worry, Jim! Monster parties have nice party food. You can eat cake and ice cream. The games are **fun**. Monsters don't really go to monster parties – and we can make a monster costume!"

Jim wasn't worried now.

Jim and Mum got a big box, a lot of paper and Mum's old coat. Jim got his paints. Then they made a monster costume.

Jim wore the costume and looked in the mirror.

"*Grrr!*" he said. "This is good! I'm a funny monster, not a scary monster!"

"You are a fantastic monster, Jim!" said Mum.

The party

It was the day of the party. Jim was worried again. But he wore his monster costume and took Tom's present. Then Jim and his mum went to Tom's house.

Jim stood outside Tom's house. Then he saw a big, scary shape inside the house.

"Oh dear! It's a monster!" thought Jim.

The door opened.

"Hello, Jim!" said the scary shape. "Come in!"
It wasn't a monster – it was Tom's dad!

"Hi, Jim! Come and play in the garden!"
said Tom.

Jim and Tom ran around the garden and had monster **races**. They played monster games and danced. Everyone liked Jim's funny monster costume.

There were **prizes** at the party, but Jim didn't **win** the prize for the best monster dance. He didn't win the prize for the fastest monster race. But Jim didn't feel sad, because the monster party was a lot of fun.

Then Tom's dad said, "Come here, Jim! You win the prize for the best monster costume!"

Jim got a big box of monster chocolates as his prize. He gave everyone a chocolate from the box.

"Thank you, Jim!" said Tom.

Then everyone sat down and ate some monster food. The monster food was very nice! Jim ate some monster cheese sandwiches and some monster chocolate cake. He drank orange juice from a monster glass.

After the monster food, they had a monster **treasure hunt**. Tom's dad hid little toy monsters in the garden: in the trees, under the flowers and behind the wall. Jim found three toy monsters!

At the end of the party, Mum took Jim home.

"Did you have **fun**, Jim?" she asked.

"Yes!" said Jim. "We had monster fun! It was the best party!"

After the party

After the party, Jim and Tom were good friends. Tom came to play at Jim's house. They went to the park after school. Jim sat next to Tom in class.

Tom always had lots of friends. Now Jim had lots of friends, too!

Then it was Jim's birthday.

"I have a great idea for a party!" he told Tom.

Jim gave Tom an invitation to ...

... a dragon party!

Come to my dragon party!
· Dragon games
· Dragon costumes
· Fantastic dragon food!

Love, Jim

Mini-dictionary

Listen and read

costume (noun) A **costume** is a set of clothes that you wear to dress as someone or something else for a party.

fun (adjective) If something is **fun**, it is nice and you like doing it.

fun (noun) If you have **fun**, you think that what you are doing is nice and it makes you happy.

invitation (noun) An **invitation** is the piece of paper you get when someone asks you to go to a party.

invite (verb) If you **invite** someone to a party, you ask them to come to it.

prize (noun) A **prize** is a special object that you give to the person who wins a game or a competition.

problem (noun) A **problem** is something that makes you worry.

race (noun) A **race** is a competition to see who is the fastest.

scary (adjective) If something is **scary**, it makes you feel afraid.

treasure hunt (noun) A **treasure hunt** is a game in which you try to find a special object by answering questions. Each question takes you to a new place, where there is another question. You keep going until you answer all of the questions.

win (verb) If you **win**, you do better than everyone else in a game or a competition.

worried (adjective) If you are **worried**, you are unhappy because you think something is wrong.

1 Look and order the story

2 Listen and say

Collins

Published by Collins
An imprint of HarperCollins*Publishers*
Westerhill Road
Bishopbriggs
Glasgow
G64 2QT

HarperCollins*Publishers*
1st Floor, Watermarque Building
Ringsend Road
Dublin 4
Ireland

William Collins' dream of knowledge for all began with the publication of his first book in 1819.

A self-educated mill worker, he not only enriched millions of lives, but also founded a flourishing publishing house. Today, staying true to this spirit, Collins books are packed with inspiration, innovation and practical expertise. They place you at the centre of a world of possibility and give you exactly what you need to explore it.

© HarperCollins*Publishers* Limited 2020

10 9 8 7 6 5 4 3 2

ISBN 978-0-00-839739-5

Collins® and COBUILD® are registered trademarks of HarperCollins*Publishers* Limited

www.collins.co.uk/elt

British Library Cataloguing in Publication Data

A catalogue record for this publication is available from the British Library.

Author: Catherine Baker
Illustrator: Dusan Pavlic (Beehive)
Series editor: Rebecca Adlard
Commissioning editor: Zoë Clarke
Publishing manager: Lisa Todd
Product managers: Jennifer Hall and Caroline Green
In-house editor: Alma Puts Keren
Project manager: Emily Hooton
Editor: Matthew Hancock
Proofreaders: Natalie Murray and Michael Lamb
Cover designer: Kevin Robbins
Typesetter: 2Hoots Publishing Services Ltd
Audio produced by id audio, London
Reading guide author: Emma Wilkinson
Production controller: Rachel Weaver
Printed and bound by: GPS Group, Slovenia

MIX
Paper from responsible sources

FSC www.fsc.org
FSC™ C007454

This book is produced from independently certified FSC™ paper to ensure responsible forest management.

For more information visit: **www.harpercollins.co.uk/green**

Download the audio for this book and a reading guide for parents and teachers at www.collins.co.uk/839739